T
Cr

B
S

Southwark
Council

DULWICH LIBRARY
368 Lordship Lane
London SE22 8NB

www.southwark.gov.uk/libraries 🐦 @SouthwarkLibs

10654452

Please return/renew this item
by the last date shown.
Books may also be renewed by
phone and Internet.

by Lisa Rajan
Eerika Omiyale

When Tara Binns runs widdershins
Around the costume box,
The attic spins, the fun begins,
The magic clasp unlocks.

"Widdershins?
What's widdershins?"
Both you and Tara say,
It's when you run in circles
But go round the other way.

The box has big ideas,
And lots of hats and shoes,
It puts her in a costume
She wouldn't normally choose.

Each outfit brings adventure,
And takes her far away,
She shuts her eyes and wonders
"What will I be today?"

She's wearing navy overalls,
The dust cloud starts to clear,
Protective goggles on her eyes,
She's now an engineer.

She's working in a factory
That makes a family car,
Her job is testing brakes and tyres
To see how safe they are.

She holds a yellow clipboard,
With a pencil on a string,
And sits by a computer
That can work out everything.

And when each car is finished,
It's Tara's job to test
Which tyres grip the road most
And which brake pads work the best.

One car's brakes aren't working,
And it rolls towards a wall!
Tara tries to stop it,
But trips up and has a fall.

"Ouch! My wrist is hurting,
And I think I've grazed my knees,
My leg is really painful
Will somebody help me please?"

DANGER! ELECTRICITY

12:03

A voice says "Hi, I'm Molly,
I hope you are OK,
I know how much it hurts
When you hit the ground that way".

"The car has crashed! The bumper
Is all crumpled", Tara said,
"But something saved the dummy
From a big bump on the head!"

"The airbag!" shouted Molly,
"Engineered with such precision,
That it inflates really quickly
When the car has a collision."

"A cushion full of air
Between the driver and the wheel,
Protects his head from injury,
And all the pain he'd feel."

"How clever!" pondered Tara,
"I wish I could insert
Airbags into my trouser legs -
Then falling wouldn't hurt."

"Inflating coats and trousers!
A brilliant idea!"
Said Tara "They would be
A clever thing to engineer!"

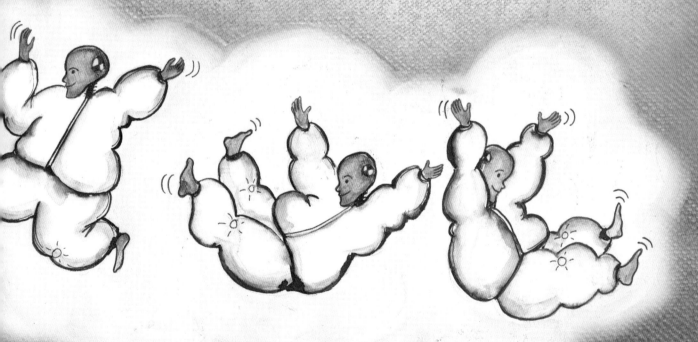

She fetched her pen and sketchpad,
And started to design
How air pumps, cloth, some tubes
And impact sensors could combine.

The finished sketch looked awesome
And above it Tara wrote:
"THE WORLD'S FIRST AIRBAG TROUSERS!!
(and with matching gloves and coat)".

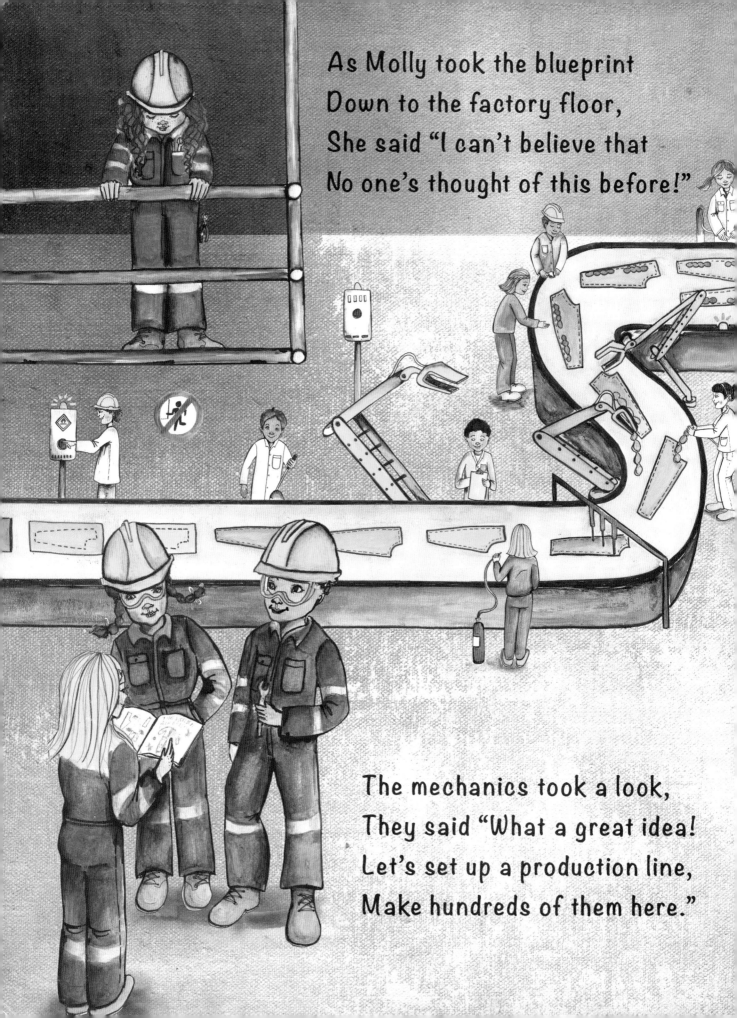

As Molly took the blueprint
Down to the factory floor,
She said "I can't believe that
No one's thought of this before!"

The mechanics took a look,
They said "What a great idea!
Let's set up a production line,
Make hundreds of them here."

The robots started working,
The lights flashed off and on,
And very soon they'd made
A pair for each and every one.

"I wonder if they work?"
Said Tara, pulling on a pair,
"Molly – trip me up – we've got
To find out how they fare."

So Tara started running,
She moved with grace and ease,
And when Molly stuck her foot out
She crash-landed on her knees.

But as she hit the concrete,
The material inflated,
The impact caused a cushion
Of warm air to be created.

It gave her a soft landing
From that very nasty fall,
The trousers had protected her,
Her knees weren't hurt at all!

"It works! It works!" said Tara,
"A brilliant breakthrough!
Not just an engineer,
Now I'm a great inventor too!"

Tara said "Let's take them out
To every park and playground,
To every child who hops and skips
And jumps and runs around".

Molly gave out trousers,
And also coats and gloves,
She said "They're great inventions
That everybody loves".

"Every child and parent will
Be singing out your praises,
No more tears at playtime now,
And no more cuts and grazes!"

And then Tara discovered,
If you change the tubes around,
And clap the gloves together
The air blasts to the ground.

The coat acts like a jet pack,
You clench your fists to steer,
You hover like a hummingbird,
Wow — what a cool idea!

The children blasted upwards,
And followed Tara Binns,
They flew around the roundabout,
And went round widdershins.

The playground started spinning,
She heard a loud KA-BOOM!!
And next thing she was back home
In that dusty attic room.

She took the overalls off and
Put the goggles in the chest,
She thought of her adventure,
And which bits she'd liked the best.

"I think that when I grow up
I will be an engineer,
Inventing new inventions —
Bigger better ones each year."

The chest replied "You kids should
All come up with something new,
Solve problems, make things better,
And make all your dreams come true".

When Tara Binns runs widdershins...

she gets to do amazing things!

In EAGLE-EYED PILOT...
she finds herself at the controls of a jumbo jet, and in avoiding a terrible thunderstorm happens upon what MIGHT be an old pirate treasure map.

In DOUBLE CHOC DOC...
she becomes a doctor, and after seeing her patients suffer with coughs, colds and sneezes, Tara goes in search of a cure... and finds one in the unlikeliest of places.

CAVENDISH ✲ KEBLE

Published by Cavendish Keble Ltd, 9 Perseverance Works, Kingsland Road, London E2 8DD, UK. All rights reserved.
First published in 2015 in the United Kingdom.

A catalogue record for this book is available from the British Library.

ISBN 978-0-9930082-1-4
Text copyright © Lisa Rajan 2015
Illustrations copyright © Cavendish Keble Ltd 2015